Lola Hopscotch and the First Day of School

by

Marie Whittaker

D1609426

The Adventures of Lola Hopscotch
Book 1

Petrichor Press
An imprint of Amity Studios

Petrichor Press

Amity Studios, LLC

Dedication

To Cody Allen and Kaitlann Marie

with all my heart.

"Lola Hopscotch is a wonderful and important book. Learning about bullying at an early age is crucial for healthy and happy kids. Everyone needs this book!"

—Jonathan Maberry, *NY Times* bestselling author

"Lola Hopscotch and the First Day of School is a wonderful tool for parents to help teach their children that it's okay to be different and help open a conversation with their child about issues they may face in school and everyday life! It's a quick, easy read that will keep a child's attention and sends a message that we can ALL relate to. I highly recommend this book and look forward to many more of Marie's stories for OUR kids!"

—Kirk Smalley, President Stand For the Silient www.standforthesilent.org

Thanks & Acknowledgments

Many thanks to this list of supporters for Lola Hopscotch and the anti-bullying project. My deepest gratitude to all of you for helping me to bring this book to life.

Kevin J. Anderson
Eloise Ruth Auld
Chef Avenue
Geoffrey Burke
David Butler
Jennifer Caress
Matt Cobham
The Creative Fund
Dawn
Ruthann DeMille
Ronin Märchen Eidolon
John Evans
David Farland
Allison Gray
Hal Greene
The Greenspon Family
Tanya Hales
John G. Hartness
Tara Henderson
Amanda Houk
Cindy Hung
Kevin Ikenberry
Mitchell Johnson
Chris Kjeldsen

Mia Kleve
Mark Leslie
Terri Locke
Jonathan Maberry
Terry Maulhardt
Christopher James Mayer
Morgen
Frank Morin
Wulf Moon
James A. Owen
Adrienne Perkins
Jennifer Peterson
Diann T. Read
Aysha Rehm
Ava and Charlie Richardson
Heather E. Robyn
Patric Ryan
Joshua Simcox
Dean Wesley Smith
Carolyn Ivy Stein
Chris Vines
Trisha J. Wooldridge
Jessica Young

Once there was a sunny meadow where buttercups bloomed and willowy sweet grass swayed. A family of lop-eared rabbits lived there, happily snug in a borough beneath a briar rose thicket.

Momma Rabbit had a little bunny named Lola. Momma looked after Lola as she played away the days smelling foxglove blossoms and tansy flowers. Lola loved to chase lazy, silver-winged dragonflies.

One night at bed time Momma Rabbit told Lola about school. It began the very next day. Many children would attend school tomorrow. Lola felt anxious. She was a bashful bunny.

4

The next morning Lola woke up early. Today was the first day of school.

Lola put on her favorite bunny dress, brushed her teeth, and combed her fur. When she was ready, Momma hopped with her along the shady path beneath nodding poppies and a canopy of yarrow blossoms.

When they arrived at the school yard Momma gave her a big hug.

"You will make lots of friends today," she said. Momma sent Lola into the yard with the other children.

Lola hopped timidly, then turned to look back at Momma Rabbit, who urged her on. There were many children at school. They watched Lola hop through the school yard. Lola felt shy.

The school bell rang and the children made a line to go inside. Lola went last.

Lola sat at a desk in the back row. The teacher worked math problems. Then the teacher spelled words. Lola watched, peeking from behind a book.

Lola was too shy to play at recess time. She sat on the school steps and watched the other children run and chase.

A young turtle and a kitten came close to where Lola sat.

"Your ears are too big," said the turtle.

"And your feet, too," said the kitten. "Much too big."

Lola smoothed the ends of her floppy ears, then looked at her bunny feet. Her feet were just right for hopping. Her ears were just right for hearing even the quietest sound.

The kitten and turtle laughed and pointed at Lola.

Lola was confused and sad. She wanted to run away when the other children began to laugh. Tears pooled in her eyes, but she did not run away.

They laughed and laughed.

"My ears are not too big," said Lola. She was surprised by her own courage. "And my feet are just the right size. Bunnies need good feet to hop and large ears to listen. It is very important."

The kitten made a rotten face at Lola. The turtle blinked and lifted his shoulders in a very slow shrug.

Lola hopped away from them.

Lola was sad to be alone, but happy she stood up for herself and disagreed with the turtle and the kitten. She sat down in the grass next to an outcropping of dainty bellflowers.

"Who-oo are you?" a little owl asked.

Lola took a deep breath. "I'm Lola Hopscotch," she said, quietly.

"I am Oliver. I am an owl. See my wings?" The little owl spanned his wings wide. Lola was surprised at how big the little owl's wings were.

A tall, grey squirrel stood beside Oliver. The squirrel had the biggest, fluffiest tail Lola had ever seen. "Siggy," squeaked the squirrel. "That's my name."

"Let's play!" squeaked Siggy.

"Lola Hopscotch, do you like to play hopscotch?" called Oliver. He made a lane of boxes with sticks. Siggy found three stones.

Lola was happy. She liked to play hopscotch very much.

They played and laughed. The other children watched.

Lola was very good at the game. She hopped far and spun fast with her bunny feet. She held out her long ears for balance when she picked up her stone.

"May I play?" asked the young turtle.

"Me, too?" asked the kitten.

"Of course," said Oliver.

Siggy nodded. A lot.

Lola nodded, too.

But the turtle did not hop-spin well at the end of the hopscotch lane. And the kitten could not throw her stone in the boxes to get started.

"May I show you how?" asked Lola. Then she showed the kitten how to toss a stone. She helped the turtle hop into the right box.

"I'm sorry I said your feet are too big," said the kitten.

"I'm sorry I said your ears are too big, too," said the turtle.

Lola smoothed her long lop-ears. "They are different than yours but perfect for me."

Lola was happy to see Momma Rabbit waiting for her after school.

"How was the first day of school? asked Momma.

"Lola remembered being sad. "It was okay. Our teacher is very nice."

"I'm glad you like your teacher," said Momma." I want to hear about everything and everyone."

They hopped home to their borough beneath the briar rose thicket, watching bumbles on bull thistles along the way.

That night as moonflowers glowed in the starry twilight and evening primroses stretched their delicate petals into the dusky nightfall, Momma tucked Lola into bed.

"Did you meet anyone you would like to tell me about at school today?"

Lola said, "Today a kitten and a turtle made fun of my feet and my ears because they're bigger than theirs. I was sad, but then we played. Maybe we will be friends."

"Everyone is different and perfect just like you, Lola Hopscotch. I'm happy you told me about the other children. I'm proud of you." Momma kissed Lola goodnight. "Let's talk again tomorrow. Dream sweet," she said.

"I'll dream of fawn lilies and fairy slippers." said Lola.

And she did just that.

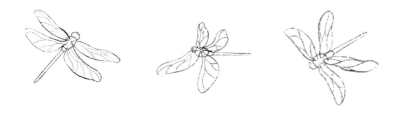

Author Biography

Marie Whittaker is an award-winning essayist and cross-genre author of genre fiction and children's books and short stories.

She created The Adventures of Lola Hopscotch book series, which is intended to foster communication between adults and children about sensitive social issues.

She has enjoyed professions as a truck driver, bar tender, and raft guide, and now works as Associate Publisher at a mid-sized, new-model press and directs a world-class conference for writers each year. A Colorado native, Marie resides in Manitou Springs, where she enjoys renovating her historical Victorian home. She spends time hiking, gardening, and trying to quit wasting time on social media. A lover of animals, Marie is an advocate against animal abuse and assists with lost pets in her community. Find her
at www.mariewhittaker.com.

www.lolahopscotch.com

How can YOU help other kids that have been bullied?

Made in the USA
Coppell, TX
29 March 2021